A Father's World

Presented to:

_____

_____

By:

_____

_____

_____ 19 _____

A Father's World

Leroy Brownlow

Photography by Robert Cushman Hayes

BROWNLOW PUBLISHING COMPANY, INC.

P. O. Box 3141

Fort Worth, Texas 76105

Brownlow Gift Books

Contents

I

No Matter What You Call Him

A father may be wealthy and prominent and his children wish to designate him with an appellation of awe and thus call him *"Father."* If he tills the soil or teaches a Bible class, they may consider it appropriate to call him *"Pa."*

Father's disposition may be such that he likes to sit in shirt sleeves, with open collar, at ball games and picnics, and nothing suits him better than to be called *"Pop."*

He may have a special talent for wheeling the baby carriage and carrying bundles meekly, and his children call him *"Papa"* with the accent on the first syllable.

If he belongs to a scientific guild or a literary association and writes scholarly papers, or if he is a reformer in our society, his family may prefer to call him *"Papa"* with the accent on the last syllable.

If, however, he is a genuine pal to his children, one to whom they feel perfectly free to go with their problems, and at the same time is too smart to let them pull the wool over his eyes, they may wish to call him *"Dad"* and he loves it.

No matter what you call him, in most cases he is the embodiment of all the characteristics mentioned above, at least to some degree, and to his children no one has quite so fine a father as they. This is the way it is and this is the way it should be. So in expressing their true feelings they would have to use one long hyphenated word that includes every name we have mentioned: Father-Pa-Pop-Papa-Papa-Dad.

And there is another name for some fathers: grandfather. Solomon said, "Children's children are the crown of old men." The very word (grand father) speaks volumes. They are old enough to realize that the newly-arrived child from the hand of God is a link between two worlds. Grandfather can especially enjoy the childish sweetness, warm companionship and wide-eyed adoration of the grandchild without feeling so much the weighty responsibility and care which rested on him as he was rearing his own children. Never will a man stand any higher, or be any greater, than he is in the eyes of his grandchild.

• *Regardless of the charming name you call father, he gave his children theirs.* Whether it be Jones, Smith, Brown or any one of a thousand others, it is a precious and laudable possession. There is no heritage more valuable than a good name. A name can be made to stand for character, qualities and virtues. It can be a synonym for whatsoever things are honest and lovely and of good report.

"A good name is rather to be chosen than great riches, and loving favor rather than silver and gold" (Proverbs 22:1).

• *Father is a man whose most sacred trust is the rearing of children,* call him the endearing name you will. Children have many needs and one of the most urgent is training, so God gave them father and mother.

Flowers, music and children are three of the most beautiful things in this world. Every flower has harmony of color which appeals to the eye. Music has harmony of sound which appeals to the ear. And childhood has harmonies of truth, purity and nobility which appeal to the heart.

The prettiest flowers and the sweetest music and the best children are made by cultivation. The wild rose is beautiful, but not as pretty as the cultivated one in the garden. Amateurs can make stirring music, but it is not in the class with that made by the master musician whose native ability became genius by dedicated and patient practice. The most fragrant flowers do not grow wild and the most enrapturing music does not just happen. It takes the mind and hand of cultivation to bring out the best.

Solomon applied the same principle to rearing children when he said, "Train up a child in the way he should go: and when he is old, he will not depart from it" (Proverbs 22:6). The child should receive intellectual, physical, religious and social rearing. Jesus did. He increased in wisdom and stature and in favor with God and man" (Luke 2:52). Teaching the highest principles form the highest character. We know:

> As the twig is bent,
> The tree's inclined.

A father's training his children is the world's highest calling for any man. In speaking of his home state, Daniel Webster once said, "Our soil is poor; we cannot produce great crops, but we raise men." That is the greatest achievement of all. It is a service that is im-

mortal. Perhaps not even fathers themselves can under-
stand the full value and extensive impact of their humble
work of rearing youth. Edward Markham, however,
caught a little vision of it and left for others his
thoughts in this poem:

> We are all blind until we see
>   That in the human plan
> Nothing is worth the making if
>   It does not make the man.
> Why build these cities glorious
>   If man unbuilded goes?
> In vain we build the work unless
>   The builder also grows.

● *Father's duties are strenuous,* regardless of the loving name you use to designate him. Nature does not
spare him. His burdens are heavy.

Heading a household is a big task, and this is one of his
jobs. "For the husband is the head of the wife, even
as Christ is the head of the church . . ." (Ephesians
5:23). Any person who has to make decisions has a
heavy burden.

Providing for his family, especially in a society where
the standards are so high, is a life-ebbing task. The span
of life is shorter for men than women. This obligation
imposed upon him, mentioned in the Holy Bible, weighs
heavily upon his heart: "But if any provide not for his
own, and specially for those of his own house, he hath
denied the faith, and is worse than an infidel" (I Timothy
5:8).

Though his duties are multiplied and exacting, he
reaches down into his heart and comes up with the
courage to look them in the face and say, "I can."

> So nigh is grandeur to our dust,
>   So near is God to man,
> When duty whispers low, 'Thou must.'
>   Father replies, 'I can.'

His fatigue is often evident and there are good reasons
for his weariness. His hands are busy. His mind is oc-
cupied with planning. His soul goes out to his children,
the objects of his solicitude. After many years of brave
and victorious bearing up under stress and strain, wear
and tear, nature begins to exact her penalty which is all
too visible. But this is living at its best, though it has a
thousand cares. Everything in this world must give way
to time and wear. However, across over in heaven where
families hope to be reunited, it will be different.
"Eternity has no gray hairs. The flowers fade, man
grows old and dies, the world lies down in the sepulchre
of ages, but time writes no wrinkles on the brow of
eternity." — Bishop Heber.

• *He is good* whether you call him "Father," "Pa,"
"Papa" or "Dad." His goodness is self-revealing and is
like a rose which cannot be hidden. Even though the
rose is unseen in your pocket, people know you have it.
It sheds fragrance; and like the rose, lofty goodness will
come out. Father's goodness makes its presence known.
Once in crossing a meadow we came to a place that was
filled with fragrance. Yet no flowers were to be seen,
and we wondered from whence came the sweet aroma.
At last, down close to the ground, we found beneath the
tall grass innumerable flowers in bloom. They could
not be concealed.

> Father's goodness is so sweet,
>   And shy, hidden like the humble flowers,
> We pass him by, with our careless feet,

> Nor dream 'tis his fragrance fills the bower,
> And cheers and comforts us by the hour.

• *Father's being young or old has no bearing on the preciousness of the name his children call him.* It does not make any difference how young or old he is, he is still a friend on your side—yea, more than a friend—and we love him for it. We do not care how many wrinkles he may have or how his rheumatism makes him limp or how the gray colors his hair, he is still the same great man and the object of our love and adoration.

As the Bible points out, the years have given him renewed youth on the inside. "For which cause we faint not; but though our outward man perish, yet the inward man is renewed day by day" (II Corinthians 4:16). In spite of the accumulation of the burdens of many years and the long road he has traveled, he found a renewal of youth and soared like an eagle, ran and was not weary, walked and did not faint. "But they that wait upon the Lord shall renew their strength; they shall mount up with wings as eagles; they shall run, and shall not be weary; and they shall walk, and not faint" (Isaiah 40:31). His "youth is renewed like the eagle's"; so this is why he has never seemed old.

• *He is an ideal,* no matter what you call him. That ideal is aptly stated in the poem:

AN IDEAL

I wish I were as big a man,
  As big a man,
  As bright a man,
I wish I were as right a man in all this earthly show,
As broad and high and long a man,

As strong a man,
  As fine a man,
As pretty near divine a man as one I used to know.

I wish I were as grave a man,
  As brave a man,
As keen a man,
As learned and serene a man, as fair to friend and foe;
I wish I owned sagaciousness
  And graciousness,
  As should a man
Who hopes to be as good a man as one I used to know.

I'd be a creature glorious,
  Victorious,
  A wonder-man,
Not just-as-now-a blunder man whose ways
And thoughts are slow,
  If I could only be the man,
  One-half of one degree the man,
I used to think my father was, when I was ten or so.

—Benton Braley

II

Honor Father

ONE of the ancient duties enjoined upon mankind is to honor parents. This age-old injunction is one of the Ten Commandments in the Old Testament: "Honor thy father and thy mother: that thy days may be long upon the land which the Lord thy God giveth thee" (Exodus 20:12).

This command was later included in the sublime and moving instructions given by the apostle Paul in the New Testament (Ephesians 6:2, 3).

Here is a command old in origin, but just as new in its essentiality and appropriateness as ever. It is the urgent need for each new generation. Man can no more outgrow his need of this respectful relationship than he can outgrow his need of basic character. To try to build a character without it is like trying to build a house without a foundation.

● *Even God has crowned man with honor:* "What is man, that thou are mindful of him? . . . For thou hast made him a little lower than the angels, and hast crowned him with glory and honor" (Psalms 8:4, 5). Thus it is especially fitting and godly that a child crown his own earthly father with honor. It is evident that humanity is not a thing to be trifled with. This thought should stir our hearts with awe and wonder.

● *Father's human imperfection is no argument against*

honoring him. Sometimes children see only a father's faults and then philosophically reason that this frees them of all duty to respect him who begot them in his own image. Yes, he has faults, but so has mother and so has son and so has daughter. "For all have sinned and come short of the glory of God" (Romans 3:23). So the faults are not all on one side.

Children sometimes falsely reason: "I should not be expected to honor my father any more than he can command. If he has not my choice of qualities which automatically move me to esteem him, why should I respect him? I am now mature and the mere fact that he happens to be my father is no more reason for honoring him than any one else unless I feel it."

Hold on! That may seem philosophical and reasonable. But suppose we turn the tables. Just suppose that when you came into the world a helpless, crying baby to disturb the routine and quiet of his life he had reasoned in the same cold and judicial vein. Suppose he had looked you over with a critical eye and a cold heart and said, "This child is unattractive and unpromising. He has disagreeable habits and is not congenial to me. I do not see in him qualities which inspire my love. Why should I be under obligation to the child just because I happen to be his father?"

Sons and daughters everywhere, it was fortunate for you that nearly all fathers and all worthy of the name have had a warmer, kinder, more unselfish and loftier attitude toward you. Your life would have been quite different, if it had not been for the love which welled up in the depth of his big paternal heart. And it is a poor rule that does not work both ways.

• *Flagrant disregard of the divine law to honor father has in it the seeds of frustration and disorder, violence and degradation.*   It produces a mischievous self-assertion and a bitter resentment of all authority and superiority. Sociologists and criminologists are now beginning to say that the cure for juvenile delinquency is to put father back at the head of the family and to honor him as such.

Disrespect, ingratitude and neglect toward father is a monstrous, deadly force which destroys individual character, which in turn pulls down our whole social structure; for the family is the cornerstone of society.

The family cannot exist and fulfill its mission without honor to its head and filial submission to his authority. Affection, devotion and respect to father are cardinal virtues, and a society divested of them cannot long survive. If children are devoid of them, they are destitute of both heart and honor.

• *We honor father because the years have taught us that he is much more deserving of honor than we could appreciate when we were in our teens.*

This thought was aptly expressed by the great American humorist, Mark Twain. He said that when he was sixteen years old he thought his father was just about the dumbest man he had ever seen. Then when he became twenty-six he decided his father was very brilliant, and he wondered how the old man had learned so much in only ten years.

Truth is mighty and will prevail. Youth must grow up. The years season youth into manhood and womanhood. Time is an effectual teacher. The years are wrought with strong opposition, serious setbacks and staggering blows from a world which looks to youth easy to conquer. Sons and daughters may not learn this until the old man is dead and gone, but here is one thing sure—they will learn.

And all the while nature is planning a sweet revenge. By and by those children will grow up and have children of their own, and the drama of parents and children is re-enacted all over again. The difference is the characters are changed and he who was the son is now the father.

● *Father is worthy of honor because he bridged many chasms for our progress in life's perilous road.* So much of what he did was not for himself but for his family. He took the bumps along the road to make traveling easier for his children. His road was marked with gorges and when safely across on the other side he turned around and built bridges for younger and less-experienced feet to have a firmer footing. Dad was a bridge builder.

THE BRIDGE BUILDER

An old man, going a lone highway,
Came at the evening, cold and gray,
To a chasm, vast and deep and wide,
Through which was flowing a sullen tide.
The old man crossed in the twilight dim—
That sullen stream held no fears for him;
But he turned, when he reached the other side,
And built a bridge to span the tide.

"Old man," said a fellow pilgrim near,
"You are wasting your strength in building here.
Your journey will end with the ending day;
You never again will pass this way.
You have crossed the chasm, deep and wide,
Why build you this bridge at eventide?"

The builder lifted his old gray head.
"Good friend in the path I have come," he said,
"There followeth after me today,
A youth whose feet must pass this way.
This chasm that has been as naught to me
To a fair-haired youth may a pitfall be.
He, too, must cross in the twilight dim;
Good friend, I'm building this bridge for him."

—William Droomogoole

• *We honor father because he clings to his children to the very last, if he is a true father.* He loves his children not because everything in them is lovely and according to his liking, but because there is a real incomprehensible bond which is stronger than fiction. He loves his children as God loves us, not because we are sinless, but because we are his children. The Bible says that God loved us while we were yet sinners, and so does the earthly father love his children in spite of their faults.

The relation of child to father is beautiful, strong and sacred. It is so filled with love and solicitude that God used the earthly type of fatherhood to teach us the true nature of man's relationship to Himself.

• *Father deserves honor because of his practical experience.* Tried by the years, he has gained knowledge from success and failure. It may not be book learning or new ideas; but it is knowledge just the same and the kind, after all, that is the most useful and worthwhile. It is practical knowledge because it discerns the morally right and wrong in life, the good and evil in the world, the building up and tearing down of character, the path to happiness and the road to despair.

He may be a humble man who never enjoyed the advantages of a formal education, but the chances are nearly everything he says to his children about their going to school, their work, their habits of play, their handling of money, their choice of friends, their choice of reading materials, their being out late at night, their reading their Bible and their going to church, is right and right beyond question.

• *A remembrance of father's sacrifices rekindles in our hearts the disposition to do him honor.* Different fathers are compelled to rear their children under different circumstances, but the same feeling in the heart is universal.

Maybe father was denied the privileges of education and social culture. Maybe he is poor as the world counts riches, but there is a man that counts more. His hands are coarse and calloused, but they are as tender and sensitive to his children's needs as ever equipped a human being. His speech is ungrammatical, but his thoughts are none the less wise. I have heard my father say, "A cat with a silver collar is none the better mouser." So a thought dressed up in perfect grammar and eloquent words is none the more profound.

He has a child or two or three or more in whose lives and happiness his own life and happiness are bound up. He wants them in higher, more useful and more comfortable positions than he has ever known—details are unnecessary. You know the story of sacrifice— rigorous toil, long hours, maybe two jobs, unremitting thrift, the slow accumulation of savings, at times bitter discouragement, but eventually the outpourings of happiness which sprang from his heart as he began to see the realization of his hopes for his children. "O Lord, by these things men live."

In some cases the father is rich and educated. By native ability and training, application and strength of character, he has made his way and his fortune in the world, but not without paying the price. There are too many obstacles in man's path to think that fame and fortune come easily, barring a few exceptions. The world sees the glitter of the gold and not the sweat of the sacrifices of him who wielded the pick in yonder mountainside. The world sees the glories of an education, but not the thousand volumes which propped up drooping eyelids at midnight hours while others peacefully slept in dreamland. Achievement always demands its sacrifices and takes its toll.

While a father's mind may be filled with education and his purse packed with money, even though it is uncommon for him to have both, his heart knows the same emptiness and the same throes for his children as all other men in other circumstances. Human nature is the same. Every heart must fight its own battles. While it costs no material hardships for the rich man to educate his children, as it does the poor man, the feelings in the heart are the same. The love, the joy, the anticipation are the same, for both are human. The same sharp sword pierces the hearts of both the rich and the poor when their children suffer.

This feeling is a savor in our society. And the friends of humanity will do all in their power to encourage the child to reciprocate and to incline him toward a thoughtful recognition of his duty to honor father.

● *We esteem father because of his heroism.* His sweat and tears and blood, shed for us, testify to his heroic nature; for he who struggles for others when the easy way is to run is a hero, call him what you will.

We have been woefully negligent of the heroic father who takes the wounds of the everyday struggles of life. We are protected because he bravely dared. The highest and noblest spirit is "that a man may lay down his life for another." Father did this not in one supreme gift, but in the giving of himself little by little, day by day. The daily conflicts of earning a living and heading a household brought out the slumbering qualities of the hero.

> Not at the battle front merit of in story,
> Not in the blazing wreck, steering to glory;
> Not while in martyr-pangs soul and flesh sever,
> Lives he—this Hero now; hero forever.
>
> —James Braidwood

The spirit of patriotism nerves the arm of the warrior and fortifies the heart of the soldier. Love of country is a powerful thing, but stronger is the love of:

Home, Sweet Home

Some of us today carry in our hearts the emptiness that was left when father moved into the promised land. The hurt is not as deep as it once was, but the void is there. We can now do nothing for him directly. Oh, but if the hands on the clock of time could be turned backward! How inexpressibly sweet would be every fulfillment of the duty to honor father. But it is vain to wish for a return of opportunities we too lightly esteemed when we had them. All that is left for us

now is to honor his hallowed memory, his name and the guiding principles he taught us. We can pay tribute to father by being the kind of children we ought to be. This reflects honor upon him.

We say to father, living or dead, your deeds, your unselfish deeds, your glorious deeds, shall never die. They shall ever be hallowed in the cherished memory of grateful children who dedicate themselves anew to the blessed privilege of honoring father.

III

What It Means to Be a Father

GRANDER than any dream is the glorious destiny to one for whom the bells of fatherhood toll. It means much, so much that even fathers themselves will never be able to fully comprehend its breadth and length, depth and height.

• *God provided for humanity's need by giving us father and mother.* "So God created man in his own image, in the image of God created he him; male and female created he them" (Genesis 1:27). Then the wise God said, "Therefore shall a man leave his father and his mother, and shall cleave unto his wife: and they shall be one flesh" (Genesis 2:24). Herein we see the provision for the family unit through which there is to be the pro-creation of the race with all the father and mother instinct to provide the necessary care, love and teaching for the children.

After the child is born father is urgently needed, but not an absolute necessity. Many families have had the misfortune of losing father. The blow was staggering, but they still carried on. They had more problems, but they solved them. They had more burdens, but they bore them. As much as father is needed, there is still only one necessity—God. And there is no faith like this faith. Though we perish, God abides. The world is not in our hand, but lies safe in His.

This is the acknowledgment which makes one a more excellent father.

• *Man was made the head of the family unit.* "But I would have you know, that the head of every man is Christ; and the head of the woman is the man; and the head of Christ is God" (I Corinthians 11:3). For the efficiency of the family some one had to be made the head and this solemn responsibility was placed on man. Nature itself proves that the job was given to man, not because he has any more intellect than woman, for he has not. Man with his masculine traits of unyielding firmness and robust resoluteness, however, is better prepared for the role of heading the family than the mother possessed with the gentle and emotional traits of femininity. Both sets of characteristics are needed to make the family unit complete. One without the other is insufficient.

The duty to head a family is a grave and sacred charge that must be held with creditable care and inviolate trust. It taxes the best there is in a man.

That is what it means to be a father.

• *It means one has the necessary duty of providing for more than himself.* He must provide for his family. The Bible makes it plain that this is hallowed responsibility. "But if any provide not for his own, and specially for those of his own house, he hath denied the faith, and is worse than an infidel" (I Timothy 5:8).

From the beginning of man's existence he has had to work for a living. In the long, long ago man was told, "In the sweat of thy face shalt thou eat bread, till thou return unto the ground; for out of it wast thou taken: for dust thou art, and unto dust shalt thou return" (Genesis 3:19). The history of man is the history of work. This is a workaday world.

The cravings of the body will not let us forget the need of making a living. Hunger is not to be denied too long. While the Christ knew that man should not live by bread alone he knew full well that man must live by bread.

The family is dependent on work for its daily existence and happiness. The word "work" has a most prominent and lofty place in the Bible, being mentioned more than five hundred and fifty times.

God promises no loaves to the loafer, but rather says, "If any would not work, neither should he eat" (II Thessalonians 3:10). The discerning man knows that the world does not owe him a living—it was here first.

The houses in which we live, the furniture for our comfort, the fuel that warms us, the clothes we wear, the food we eat, the schools we attend, our pleasures and our safety, have all been made possible by thinking minds and working hands.

The happiest and most efficient worker sees the wonder and beauty of labor. He sees more in his toil than a living. The baker sees not only the paycheck at the end of the week or the weariness of the job, but he sees the human family in countless homes, seated about tables and eating that bread in the joy of human companionships. The most contented shoemaker is the man who has a view beyond leather and tacks and stitches and sees the young and the old wear a necessity he provides. This takes the drudgery from labor and makes it satisfying and pleasant. So it is with father's work, regardless of the vocation, but to a much greater degree. He sees in his toil many blessings for his family. Beyond his labors he sees a picture which defies the brush of any artist to reproduce and more than challenges the pen of any author to describe.

That is what it means to be a father.

• *While father must make a living, he must also live a life.* Living is taller and deeper than the satisfaction which comes from providing only material things. Every child needs a living, but not as an end within itself. It is possible to provide luxury and ease and a display of this world's goods without laying a life on the world's altar as an uplifting force to stimulate the children to reach for a grander and nobler star.

For children to really live, they must have more than food for the body. They must have food for the mind and soul. The child is a dual being, flesh and spirit. The body is visible. Feed it. Clothe it. Though the inner being is invisible, the need to feed and clothe it is the more urgent. This clay will again turn to clay. But the influence father exerts on the child's soul, the hope he strengthens, the faith he encourages, these things will never die. This gives a greater meaning to fatherhood.

A coal miner father had a day off and decided to spend it in a nearby saloon. Slipping quietly away from home, he began walking in that direction. He had not gone far when he heard a voice behind him. It was his six-year-old son who said, "Go ahead, daddy, I'm walking in your steps." But daddy did not go right ahead. The child's remark took on a deeper and more thought-provoking significance. The father turned and picked up his little boy and said, "My foot steps are not going to lead you there."

That is what it means to be a father.

• *The loftiest of all duties is to so shape the child's mind that he may do his bit to make the world inviting for faith, hope and love.* The Bible words it this way: "And, ye fathers, provoke not your children to wrath: but bring them up in the nurture and admonition of the Lord" (Ephesians 6:4).

Father has a job of teaching to do by speaking, but not by speaking alone; by action, but not by action alone; by hoping, and by sharing that hope; by courage, and by instilling that courage in the heart of the child. Just to ponder these thoughts is the beginning of an education for both father and child. There is nothing that so educates the parent as the child.

> God has his small interpreters
> The child must teach the man.
>
> —John G. Whittier

It is an education to bear a child, provide for, train and educate him or her, and, with anxiety of soul, take the boy into your heart or hold that girl to your bosom, watching with eyes that never sleep and with a foresight that never slumbers.

That is what it means to be a father.

• *The building of character is the most valuable work of life.* No beautiful character ever grew dissociated of wise teaching and apart from uplifting influences. Words and deeds of others built character into that life. Characters are built as temples are. Some one had to work at it. Each stone was laid in its place by toil and effort, and stone by stone the building rose. And so it is of the noble edifice of character. That person you admire so much did not just dream himself into truth and love and purity. He was built skyward by effort. Building character is a matter of workmanship. It is the parents' duty to assist the child in choosing the best of materials, to be watchful of companionships, to be wise in his pleasures and to be cautious of his habits.

> Souls are built as temples are —
> Here a carving rich and quaint,
> There the image of a saint;
> Here a deep-toned pain to tell
> Sacred truth or error of hell.
> Every little helps the much;
> Every cheerful, careless touch
> Adds a charm or leaves a scar.

Characters must be built to stand storms. Storms of temptation are sure to sweep over men. Floods of evil will flow against them. If men and women are going to stand with heads skyward, then they must possess qualities and habits which hold them together.

> Sow a thought, you reap an act;
> Sow an act, you reap a habit;
> Sow a habit, you reap a character;
> Sow a character, you reap a destiny.

Experience proves that just a few repetitious thoughts create a certain mental tendency which form a habit. Habit is like the channel which dictates the course the river flows and which grows deeper year by year. Habits are like the paths people made across city lots or country fields. The path is made by being walked over again and again and again. The more we do a thing the easier it becomes.

A minister traveling in the West shook hands with an old stage driver who had fingers bent inward which he could not straighten. The old man held up his hands and suggested a sermon topic: "In these crooked fingers of mine," he said, "there is a good text for a sermon! For fifty years I drove a stage, and these bent fingers show the effects of holding the reins for so many years." When that man was a boy his fingers were as straight and limber as anyone's. But for years he held the reins with tight hands and they became set to that grip he exerted. His crooked fingers are but an emblem of the crooked tempers and dispositions which produce ugly words and actions which, when repeated over and over, become a habit.

Someone has well said, "Faults are like young spiders, little and insignificant at first, but, if let alone, they group, spin webs that accumulate dust and darken the windows of the soul through which character shines out, and deform the whole man. Better destroy the little spiders before they are old enough to spin—better correct the faults while they are small, lest they not only deform the character, but so bedim the moral vision that the soul cannot discern between truth and error, right and wrong, the noble and the ignoble in life."

Years ago my father and I and another man sailed out from Corpus Christi on the Gulf of Mexico in a small motor boat. Our destination was an island where we spent the night and fished the next day. To make sailing easier, we went out with the tide and came in with the tide. Like the tide that can help or hinder are our habits. How fortunate is the boy or girl who has a wise and thoughtful father who helps to develop the force of good habits on his or her side.

That is what it means to be a father.

• *Majestic depths of feeling are found in the word "father."* The following true experience testifies to the music and magnetism found in the word:

A little boy who was deaf was sent to a special school where he learned to partially speak. When the son returned to his home he ran to his father with stretched out arms and said, "My father." The father was overwhelmed and later commented: "If I live to be ninety, I'll never forget the moment when I heard my son say, 'My father'."

That is what it means to be a father.

• *Being a father means one has given the world an offspring to help carry on a work that he must sooner or later leave unfinished.* This is the history of the race and the story of the long evermoving procession which stretches from the cradle to the grave. No life is ever complete. The oldest man dies with his work unperformed. The early years were full of promise, marked by the radiant glow of a golden age that lay before. It is not uncommon in youth to find heroic men and beautiful women who labor with strenuous souls to make right prevail. Youth is visionary and vigorous, bold and beneficient. Blessed youth, how great you are!

But take what the youth planned and measure it by what the man years later performed and you will ordinarily find an infinite distance between. The old man who has borne the heat of the day and the burdens of the trail has been taught by the years that he is not a necessity, but only God is. He leaves his uncompleted work to be carried on by the younger man who steps into his place. Men die, but man lives. Persons pass, but the race survives. He who believes in God and man, however, can depart in peace—God abideth ever.

> Whatever dies, or is forgot—
> Work done for children dieth not.

And that is what it means to be a father.

IV

Father Found Strength Proportionate to Duty

THE profound realization that one has become a father leaves him dazed and jubilant, proud and humble. Mixed emotions fill his heart. He is now in a new world, the world of fatherhood. Just a few short years ago it was he whose hand and mind and soul reached out to receive. Now the child has become the father, and it is he whose hand and mind and soul must reach out to give. Nature has begun to balance things. And the sudden impact of a father's responsibility falls like a mountain upon him.

He is almost uncontrollably happy, but feels too big to cry. He is scared, but too brave to run. He knows this is not storybook fiction. The drama of life is real and earnest. The world is a stage and he is one of the major characters; and his role is that of father, and the way he plays his part has a bearing on success or failure for the little one. The new father is unprepared and inexperienced, clumsy and awkward. He hardly knows how to hold his own offspring. But in his weakness there is possible growth and in his feebleness there is potential power. He cries out in his heart, "God, help me"; and he finds strength proportionate to his duty.

• *Adequacy unto the requirement is one of the established laws of God and of nature.* The Bible says:

Thy shoes shall be iron and brass; and
as thy days, so shall thy strength be.
—Deuteronomy 33:25

In facing his new-born duties, father is given shoes for the march and strength for the task.

In all of nature, God gives a supply in keeping with the need.

The fish is given fins for the water; the flying bird, wings for the air; the rabbit, swift feet for the ground. The eagle understands the purpose of its talons and beak; the ant-eater, its pronged snout; and the porcupine, its quills. The camel is not afraid of the desert, because its spreading feet are a match for the sand and its extra water-tank is safety against the drouth. There are the flukes of the whale, the shell of the turtle, the spider's web and the wing-hooks of the little bat, each filling a peculiar need of its owner.

The wisely bestowed gifts to dumb creatures often change with changing requirements. The alternating seasons bring to many animals changing coats. Nature gives to the dog and the horse different coverings for summer and winter. The farther north we go the thicker we find the fur of the bear.

The principle is just as true of plant life. The plant in the cellar is the frailest because it is least called upon to stand exposure. But the tree that stands atop the mountain exposed to the wrath of the storm is the stoutest, because it found strength through trial. As the wind whipped through the branches and the trunk swayed to and fro, nature gave the tree new and needed strength by sending its roots deeper into the soil. After the storm subsided and the tree was at rest, it was firmer than ever before.

THE LAW OF LIFE

The tree that never had to fight
For the sun and sky and air and light,
That stood out in the open plain
And always got its share of rain,
Never became a forest king,
But lived and died a scrubby thing.

The man who never had to toil,
Who never had to win his share
Of sun and sky, and light and air,
Never became a manly man,
But lived and died as he began.

Good timber does not grow in ease;
The stronger wind, the tougher trees;
The farther sky, the greater length;
The more the storm, the more the strength;
By sun and cold, by rain and snows,
In trees of man, good timber grows.

Where thickest stands the forest growth,
We find the patriarch of both,
And they hold converse with the stars
Whose broken branches show the scars
Of many winds and much of strife . . .
This is the common law of life.

—Author unknown

He whose task demands the most strength is given most. He whose circumstances call for greater endurance finds his powers of fortitude increased. The blacksmith's arm grows strong, not weak, by use. Poverty's child who has no shoes becomes able to walk the flinty roads and the briary fields. Supply follows demand. Use summons strength.

You have seen the young father so transformed by the consciousness of his responsibility, so lifted to a higher sphere of thought and character, as to change his whole outward appearance in a short time. The expressions which played across his face were so mature; and his young manly form, so expanding and uplifting. As you looked at this youth turned man, you realized anew the truthfulness of this victorious principle: "As thy days, so shall thy strength be."

• *Father found strength to carry his burdens by living a day at a time.* "Sufficient unto the day is the evil thereof" (Matthew 6:34). Trying to live life in the lump brings down upon one a thousand burdens that will break any person. Trying to solve future problems which have not yet arisen will dissipate energy that should be used for present duties. Trying to cross bridges before you reach them will slow your progress. We are not against preparation for the future, but are merely suggesting that the best preparation for tomorrow is to take care of what needs to be done today. All God expects of man is to do his best today. Then he will find added strength for tomorrow's added burdens. With this philosophy, father never feared the length of the path of duty nor the flints and thorns which beset his footprints.

DAY BY DAY

I heard a voice at evening softly say,
Bear not thy yesterday into tomorrow,
Nor load this week with last week's load of sorrow.
Lift all thy burdens as they come, not try
To weigh the present with the by and by.
One step, and then another, take thy way—
    Live day by day.

• *Father gained strength for his obligations from the*

associations with his child. Loneliness is a paralyzing thing—because it engenders fear. While most of our fears come from false alarms, they are just as weakening as if the causes were real. Fear produces unsteady hands, feeble knees and a weak heart. Fear fills lonely hearts. It is the solitary soul who is fearful of the shadows. Associations with others produce courage, and courage generates strength. And there are no finer and more strengthening associations than those of parent and child. Father's fellowship with his family enhanced his might.

Father's looking upon the child's trust and faith and purity stimulated the growth of those noble traits in his own life.

THE TWO PRAYERS

Last night my little boy confessed to me
Some childish wrong;
And kneeling at my knee
He prayed with tears:
"Dear God, make me a man
Like daddy—wise and strong,
I know you can."

Then while he slept
I knelt beside his bed,
Confessed my sins,
And prayed with low-bowed head:
"O, God, make me a child
Like my child here,
Pure, guileless,
Trusting thee with faith sincere."

• *Living for others endued father with increasing power.* The life that gives itself for the good of others is always the strong life. Fatherhood provides a strong motive for self-sacrifice. He possesses a love that feels, that sympathizes and that spends itself in giving to and providing for his family. With deepest concern he enters into the condition of his child in peril and hesitates not, even at the cost of life itself, to put forth his hand to rescue. A constraining love drove self to the background.

> Love took up the harp of life,
>   And smote on all the chords with might;
> Smote the chord of self that trembling,
>   Passed in music out of sight.

In living for others, father met the condition of the larger and more fruitful life. This is true of all nature.

The little grain of wheat seems dead and silent in its husky shell. It heeds not the call of sunshine morning after morning. It stirs not as the passing clouds tell of growths and harvests to be. All wrapped in itself, it lies dormant and fruitless through the years. But in a better purpose it seeks the earth, giving self away; and then it finds within its chaff a new life, first the blade, then the blossomed ear and after that the full grown corn. In losing life, it found a new life. Christ expressed the same principle when he said, "He that loseth his life for my sake shall find it" (Matthew 10:39). The more beautiful and gracious life comes through self-sacrifice.

Father's every good deed accomplished and every worthy ambition realized not only blessed the world in which he lived, but also enriched and ennobled his own life with a treasure greater than riches and a nobility beyond all titles.

WHY DO I LIVE?

I live for those who love me;
    For those I know are true;
For the heaven that smiles above me
    And awaits my spirit too;
For all human ties that bind me,
For the task my God assigned me,
For the bright hope left behind me,
    And the good that I can do

• *Father was inspired by his children's faith and trust in him to attain new heights.* Father knows he cannot weaken because his children believe in him; he cannot falter because they trust him.

Years ago a father and a son were traveling over a dangerous mountain trail. They came to a place where a huge rock jutted out over the precipice, leaving only a hanging portion as the pathway. With much difficulty and danger, the father traversed the perilous spot. Then holding to the rock with one big hand, he reached the other out over the cliff and told the boy to step on his hand and thus pass around the rock to safety: "Do not fear to step on my hand. It is strong. It will not give way." The boy did and the hand held.

Examples which are less dramatic could be cited by the thousands. It is a common practice in the everyday struggles of life. Father extends his hand over countless precipices and chasms and says, "Step on it. It will not give way." There is too much faith in him for his big manly hand to weaken, and by more trust in it and more usage it becomes as iron.

However humble the place I may hold
  On the lowly trails I have trod,
There's a child who bases his faith in me;
  There's a dog who thinks I'm a god.

Lord, keep me worthy—Lord, keep me clean
  And fearless and undefiled,
Lest I lose caste in the sight of a dog,
  And the wide clear eyes of a child!

—C. T. Davis

V

Father's Heart

FATHER has a heart that loves, rejoices, bleeds and breaks like that of a woman, even though he may labor to withhold the visible signs. He knows from experience the meaning of all the words of any language which affect the heart. And these feelings are not peculiar to any class, color or time. They are the common lot of fathers the world over in every age and in every clime.

• *Father's heart has been misunderstood because of his reserved emotions.* One of the differences in the sexes is that man is more restrained in his emotions while woman is more effusive in hers.

Mother's place in the world's affection is secure. She has justly appealed to humanity's heart with her mother-affection, her special capacity for service, her almost unlimited devotion to duty, her gentleness and tenderness, her pain and suffering and toil, and her brooding care with caresses and tears.

Father has not so appealed to the world's imagination. Father has been endowed with more firmness, sternness and readiness for life's battles. He has to go out into the world of cold conflict where he must struggle with his burdens and strive for those he loves and for whom he would die if need be. Father . . . taking life's beatings without tears or complaints, heroically fighting his battles, grimly and steadily "carrying on" even when he knows he is waging a losing fight, but hoping and fighting and toiling as he takes the reproaches and praises with the same smiling face and unbreakable determination, rough and ready, kind and forgiving . . . has a heart of gold even though the world often fails to see it. These are the traits which make a man. They constitute the indescribable and undefinable quality which gives father the heart of a hero, call him what you will.

• *Father has a heart that can raise a firm hand or extend a tender one, as circumstances dictate.* He can be firm or soft, harsh or sympathetic, cold or compassionate. In meeting life's demands, he must be realistic and rise to the changing occasions.

> I like the man who faces what he must,
>   With step triumphant and a heart of cheer;
> Who fights the daily battle without fear.
>   —Sarah Knowles Bolton

• *To get a vivid picture of a father's heart we cite several passages from the Bible which describe him:*

> As a nursing father beareth the sucking child.
>   —Numbers 11:12

> For my father fought for you and adventured his life.   —Judges 9:17

> My father hath chastised you.   —I Kings 12:11

> And their father gave them great gifts of silver, and of gold, and of precious things.
>   —II Chronicles 21:3

> I was a father to the poor.   —Job 29:16

> My son, hear the instruction of thy father.
>   —Proverbs 1:8

For whom the Lord loveth he correcteth; even as
a father the son in whom he delighteth.

—Proverbs 3:12

A wise son maketh a glad father.

—Proverbs 10:1

The father of a fool hath no joy.

—Proverbs 17:21

A foolish son is a grief to his father.

—Proverbs 17:25

Whoso loveth wisdom rejoiceth his father.

—Proverbs 29:3

• *In the Bible we find an illustrative story of a father
who had to deal with a wayward and foolish son.* This
story perfectly describes a father's heart. The father was
a great and important king who had many worries and
problems as all kings have. Heavy hangs the head that
wears a crown. But this exalted position had no bearing
on the feelings of a true father's heart. This is one
thing about a father's heart—it knows no social, political
or monetary position. It beats the same in the breast
of the poor and rich, bond and free, peasant and king.

The father's name was David and his son's name was
Absalom. Poor Absalom! He was so cruelly misguided.
He was all mixed up. He wanted to be king so he led
a revolution against his father. He lifted a strong hand
in an effort to compensate for a weak character. He was
determined to be somebody, even if he had to climb over
his father and bleed the kingdom to do it. He could have
been somebody by just *being* somebody, but this was not
Absalom's way. His way was that of selfishness which
permitted no love for anyone except himself, and wrapped up in himself, he could see only himself. The cir-

cumstances have been different, but the tragedy of selfishness has always been the same. Selfishness! Selfishness! Thou art a friend of no one! Not even thyself!

The father had a two-fold duty to suppress and subdue the revolt. In the first place, as king it was his obligation to protect the kingdom and restore order. In the second place, as father it was his responsibility to save his son from himself. This was a most painful experience and the test of a great father's heart. There was no rancor, no bitterness, no vindictiveness, no retaliation, only tenderness and solicitude. So David made it plain to the commanding officers that his rebel son was not to be harmed. Here are some of the anxious words from a loving father's heart: "Deal gently for my sake with the young man, even with Absalom" (II Sameul 18:5). "Beware that none touch the young man Absalom" (II Sameul 18:12).

A bloody battle ensued of which the Bible says, "And there was there a great slaughter that day of twenty thousand men" (II Samuel 18:7). The revolutionary forces were routed. Absalom, while fleeing on a mule, ran under the branches of a tree and his bushy hair became entangled with the branches and left him hanging by the hair of his head. A humorous but sad spectacle: The trouble is he had not had his feet on the ground but rather his head in the air all along. His ignoble predicament was a fitting symbol of his life. Poor Absalom! Tennyson put into words the climax of his foolishness:

> Worse than being fooled
> Of others, is to fool one's self.

Absalom's dangling position was made to order in saving his life. And the first loyal soldier who found him spared his life in keeping with the king's commandment. But when General Joab, whose savagery had been stirred by the blood and excitement of the battle, was informed of the rebellious son's predicament, he immediately stated that he would not tarry with such grace. "And he took three darts in his hand, and thrust them through the heart of Absalom, while he was yet alive in the midst of the oak" (II Samuel 18:14).

David, the king and the father, anxiously waited for news of the battle. As the news began to trickle in, it is easy to see where the father's heart was. To the first messenger who brought news, David instinctively inquired first of all, "Is the young man Absalom safe?" Another runner came and again the first thing the king asked was, "Is the young man Absalom safe?"

When David learned the fate of his son, he "was much moved, and went up to the chamber over the gate, and wept: and as he went, thus he said, O my son Absalom! my son, my son Absalom! would God I had died for thee, O Absalom, my son, my son!" (II Samuel 18:33).

This reveals a father's heart. The heartbreak and the bitter blow of such a death has been described by Longfellow:

> There is no far nor near,
> There is neither there nor here,
> There is neither soon nor late,
> In that Chamber over the Gate.
> Nor any long ago
> To that cry of human woe,
>   "O Absalom, my son!"

That 'tis a common grief
Bringeth but slight relief;
Ours is the bitterest loss,
Ours is the heaviest cross;
And forever the cry will be,
"Would God I had died for thee,
O Absalom, my son!"

These moving and emotional words have been lisped by countless numbers of fathers through the ages: "My son, my son, would God I had died for thee." We have heard those words in hospital rooms as the child slipped down through the valley of the shadow of death. We have heard that wailing cry in the silent cities of the dead as broken-hearted fathers tenderly and sobbingly, yet heroically, expressed the true sentiments of the heart. The true father loves his child more than he loves himself. The father's heart beats not so much for himself as it does for his offspring. That is a father's heart.

While David had won one war he felt that he had lost another. He won the battle over the revolutionary forces, but he had lost the battle with his own son. This is often true of all of us as we wage our own life's conflicts: Though we win, we lose. But it is encouraging to recall that oftentimes the reverse is true: Though we lose, we win.

There was no victory celebration that day because the king had lost his son. The victory seemed empty. The king grieved for a foolish son, but he was his son. David's conduct seemed unrealistic to the logical, but love knows no logic. So the Bible says: "And the victory that day was turned into mourning unto all the people: for the people heard say that day how the king was grieved for his son." Here we see that a father's heart may be one of grief.

• *The demands upon father's heart are great and varied.* Our world demanded courageous minds, watchful eyes, ready hands, true faith—actually many hearts in one—and God answered the call by giving the world fathers.

Father is a man, large-hearted, manly man. The qualities of his heart seem to be a thousand hearts, and each heart an absolute necessity to fatherhood.

VI

Father and the Prodigal Son

IN what is commonly called the Parable of the Prodigal Son we are given a soul-warming, heart-stirring picture of a father's loving and merciful relationship with a foolish and wayward son. The picture is vivid and the story is gripping. Scholars the world over have applauded this narration as one of the most beautiful and thrilling stories of all literature.

• *Let us bear in mind that a real and earthly father was used to show the world a more excellent and more practical conception of our Heavenly Father.* Not all earthly fathers qualify for the place in this the loveliest of all stories, but more men nearly approach this standard of fatherhood than many are aware.

First, let us read the story as it is found in the Bible:

> And he said, A certain man had two sons: And the younger of them said to his father, Father, give me the portion of goods that falleth to me. And he divided unto them his living. And not many days after the younger son gathered all together, and took his journey into a far country, and there wasted his substance with riotous living. And when he had spent all, there arose a mighty famine in that land; and he began to be in want. And he went and joined himself to a citizen of that country; and he sent him into his fields to feed swine. And he would fain have filled his belly with the husks that the swine did eat: and no man gave unto him. And when he came to himself, he said, How many hired servants of my father's have

bread enough and to spare, and I perish with hunger!
I will arise and go to my father, and will say unto him,
Father, I have sinned against heaven and before thee,
and am no more worthy to be called thy son: make me
as one of thy hired servants. And he arose, and came
to his father. And when he was yet a great way off,
his father saw him, and had compassion, and ran, and
fell on his neck, and kissed him. And the son said
unto him, Father, I have sinned against heaven, and
in thy sight, and am no more worthy to be called thy
son. But the father said to his servants, Bring forth
the best robe, and put it on him; and put a ring on his
hand, and shoes on his feet: And bring hither the fatted calf, and kill it; and let us eat, and be merry: For
this my son was dead and is alive again; he was lost,
and is found. And they began to be merry. Now his
elder son was in the field: and as he came and drew
nigh to the house, he heard music and dancing. And
he called one of the servants, and asked what these
things meant. And he said unto him, Thy brother is
come; and thy father hath killed the fatted calf, because he hath received him safe and sound. And he
was angry, and would not go in: therefore came his
father out, and entreated him. And he answering said
to his father, Lo, these many years do I serve thee,
neither transgressed I at any time thy commandment;
and yet thou never gavest me a kid, that I might make
merry with my friends: But as soon as this thy son
was come, which hath devoured thy living with harlots,
thou hast killed for him the fatted calf. And he said
unto him, Son, thou art ever with me, and all that I
have is thine. It was meet that we should make merry,
and be glad: for this thy brother was dead, and is alive
again; and was lost, and is found.   —Luke 15:11-32

It was the younger son who asked for his part of the
inheritance. It is obvious that he was a restless, ad-
venturous boy. He was tired of home ties. He was

weary with being tied to apron strings and felt that the time had come to cut them. He was now a big boy and he could stand on his own feet without either advice or help from the home folk. No doubt he thought his father was all right, a good man, but just not bright enough for the times. This boy was ready to conquer the world, not knowing that the world was ready to conquer him.

• *And the father "divided unto them his living."* It is typical of the true father that he divided unto both sons. One did not receive while the other was denied. There was no partiality. Though this may not have been wise, the father went beyond the requirements of law and custom in an effort to hold the good will of his wayward son. He went to the utmost to keep from breaking with this headstrong boy. He doubtless thought that sharing his goods with his prodigal son would satisfy him and cause him to stay at home, at least remain in the community. But if this were the supposition, the father was wrong in it.

After a few days, the younger son gathered all his part together—no doubt turned it all into money—and journeyed into a far country where he wasted all his money in wicked prodigality. A fool and his money are soon parted, so it was not long until all the money was gone. To make it worse, a famine struck the land and this live-for-the-moment, pleasure-mad young man found himself in dire need. Nothing is said of friends, so apparently when his money was gone so were his friends. This was a cruel awakening. They were fair weather friends and now the storm had struck.

The sensible thing was for him to seek employment

and go to work. Good jobs were hard to find. Remember "there was a mighty famine in the land." Reality has to be faced and we commend the young man for facing it. If he could not get the job he wanted, then he must take the job he could get. And he did, even though it consisted of feeding swine. This boy who thought the world looked easy to take for the asking had dropped fast and hard. Now his job was to care for the hogs — quite a descent for a young man of his position and family background. It was humiliation enough to be reduced to a hog-slopper, but the more pressing agony was hunger. Even at this low task he was unable to earn a living, and he desired to eat the shucks which the hogs left and trampled in the filth and mire of the hog pen. He was starving.

The boy had acted the fool, but he was not too foolish to learn. As the whole world knows, many young people have to climb up fool's hill in order to see their mistakes and to get a broader perspective of what living is all about.

So "he came to himself." His thoughts went back to his father's old home. He remembered that he had a good father who had provided a plenteous home for him. He recalled that there was so much that the servants had bread enough and to spare while he perished with hunger.

A battle warred within him. Unfortunately and pathetically, fighting battles on the inside of himself had become his way of life. That is why he left home. That is why he gave himself to riotous living and spending. Such were only the outward manifestations of the struggle which raged within him.

• *The son's wanting to go home is an ideal tribute to the father and to the home.* It was in his father's home that he was the recipient of manifold blessings, including love, mercy, goodness and security. In that home he was somebody. And today in the home, father should be a king; mother, a queen; son a prince; and daughter, a princess.

There is power in thinking of home. "When our boys and girls go away from home today, if they leave with a mother's kiss warm upon their lips and a father's benediction fresh in their hearts, they are far better armed against temptation than the boy or the girl who has never known the sweetness of a happy home. And if they fall into sin and even go down to the brink of ruin, as long as there remains in the background of their minds the memory of a sacred home circle there is hope. There will come moments of rational reflection when they will think of that home with its family altar and its hallowed associations; they will remember the father's counsel and the mother's anxious warnings, and perhaps they will be saved through the memory of these early influences." —*Brewer's Sermons*, G. C. Brewer, p. 101.

• *We are given enough information in the story about the father to know that he surely yearned for that wandering boy to come home.* He must have prayed daily for God to bless him and send him home. "We see him in the late afternoon walking on the lawn with his hands crossed behind him and his head bowed as he meditates. Now we see him as he places one hand up above his eyes to shade them from the lowering rays of the setting sun, and looks longingly down the road in the hope that he may see his boy coming. We see him in the long winter evening as he sits before his fire and meditates in sorrow. He recalls the years when his two little boys stood by his knees and listened with wide-eyed wonder as he told them the stories of Hebrew history—the stories of Abraham and Moses, of Joshua and David. He remembers how his heart then beat high with hope that his boys would become great and good men. Then he recalls the changes that came as the boys grew up and how the younger had finally taken all his interests out of the old home and gone away. But he had continued to hope that the boy would tire of roaming and come back. He had thought he would learn his lesson and come home and settle down." —*Brewer's Sermons,* G. C. Brewer, p. 103.

● *The father's wishes came true.* The boy learned his lesson and resolved to go home. He said, "I will arise and go to my father." And surely enough the father must have been out looking for that boy, for "when he was yet a great way off, his father saw him, and had compassion, and ran, and fell on his neck, and kissed him."

The son had a little speech made up that he planned to say to his father when he got home. He wanted to say that he had sinned against his father and was no longer worthy to be called his son and was content just to be a hired servant. As you see, that boy was not all bad. It is interesting to note, however, that he never did get to make that speech. Before he could get started, the father stopped his mouth with kisses. The father's goods had been wasted, his heart had bled from the torture of anxiety and his eyes had been dimmed with the tears of disappointment; but the only thing that mattered was his son's return.

• *The father ordered the servants to bring out the best of everything for that miserable, ragged, half-starved boy.* Skip the derogatory remarks—he was his son —and he had come home. The time had come to celebrate. The father ordered that the fatted calf be killed and that they eat and be merry: "For my son was dead, and is alive again; he was lost, and is found."

• *Another interesting part of this story is to listen to the father as he reasons with the older son.* Though the elder son was a hard working boy and stayed at home, he had his weaknesses and faults, too. Selfishness and envy were his failures. When he returned from the field and heard and saw the big welcome given his brother, he had no desire to enter into the festivities. He angrily went off and pouted and sulked. The father had to go out and entreat him. That inflated older son tried to whitewash himself by rehearsing the sins of his brother. When he had finished, the father did not argue with him; he did not deny the charges; he rather reasoned with his offended boy about the propriety of the feast of honor and welcome. Listen to the father as he talks to that disturbed son:

> Son, thou art ever with me, and all that I have is thine. It was meet that we should make merry, and be glad: for this thy brother was dead and is alive again; and was lost and is found.

This story is not just one that has been told. It is one that has been lived a thousand times by fathers and sons the world over. We appreciate the son's coming to himself, and his behavior which followed is worthy of commendation. But the real hero is the father. This narrative tells us much about fathers and gives us a deeper and more profound appreciation of fatherhood. It says some things about father which need to be said again and again not only for the sake of giving honor to whom honor is due, but also for the ultimate end of bolstering our society which is so dependent upon him.

VII

Presidential Father Commends the Bible to Youth

THE material in this chapter was given in a bacalaureate sermon preached by President Zachary Taylor. He was the twelfth president of the United States. He had one son and five daughters.

Here is an imperial utterance, which peals like a trumpet: "The word of our God shall stand forever" —Isaiah 40:8.

• *This is not an isolated or accidental statement; it is representative.*

The Apostle Peter speaks of "the word of God which liveth and abideth forever."

Through the mouth of the prophet, Jehovah says: "As the rain cometh down and the snow from heaven, and returneth not thither, but watereth the earth and maketh it bring forth and bud, that it may give seed to the sower and bread to the eater, so shall my word be that goeth forth out of my mouth; it shall not return unto me void, but it shall accomplish that which I please, and it shall prosper in the thing whereto I send it."

And sitting with His disciples on the Mount of Olives, contemplating the passing of the old city so that one stone should not be left upon another, Jesus asserted the stability of the word: "Heaven and earth shall pass away, but my word shall not pass away."

● *It seems a wonderful thing that God should speak in the language of man, that words should go forth out of his mouth.* There is a sense in which all nature is vocal with truth and beauty. To the devout soul the waters may speak of refreshment, and the lands of bounty; the mountains may tell of stability, and the rocks of endurance; the glinting sunlight may whisper of gladness, and the evening shadows of gloom. In harmony with the Psalmist, Addison sings:

> The spacious firmament on high,
> And all the blue ethereal sky,
> And spangled heavens, a shining frame,
> Their great Original proclaim.

Paul declares that God hath not left himself without witness, in that he did good and gave rain from heaven and fruitful seasons, filling our hearts with food and gladness. From the tiny blade of grass that falls before the scythe to the vast orbs that hang upon nothing and sweep through the infinitudes of space, every object in creation and every phenomenon in nature has its appropriate lesson.

It is written: "Ask now the beasts and they shall teach thee, the fowls of the air and they shall tell thee; or speak unto the earth and it shall teach thee, the fishes of the sea and they shall declare unto thee." These all atest the reality and power of God, and proclaim his wisdom and fidelity; but they bring no definite disclosure of the divine will or purpose concerning the race.

● *The stability of the Word is a matter of supreme importance.* No man hath seen God at any time; and no man hath ascended up to heaven, but he that came down from heaven. The dusty mummies have slept in their narrow beds, and have waited in vain for a trumpet of resurrection. The fathers have fallen to sleep from age to age, leaving only silence and emptiness behind, while new generations have followed on to fill the void. Not a spirit of our best beloved has returned from the echoless shore to break the stillness and scatter the gloom with a reassuring word.

In vain have the most excursive intellects striven to dispel the darkness. Plato guesses, and Socrates ventures forward because he must; the laws of nature are stern, and the poison hemlock kills. Systems of philosophy are chiefly opinions of men, and though sometimes bathed in tears and blood they are opinions still. With vaulting ambition giant minds,

> Like Noah's weary dove,
>   Have soared the earth around,
> And not a resting place above
>   The cheerless waters found.

• *Only the Word of God reveals the way of life and immortality.* Only one voice testifies: "I am the resurrection and the life; he that believeth on me though he were dead yet shall he live, and he that liveth and believeth on me shall never die." From only one mouth goes forth the word: "The Lord reigneth, let the earth rejoice; let the many isles be glad thereof."

That word is the foundation of our noblest sentiments, our holiest hopes; and if the foundations be destroyed, what shall the righteous do? What shall it profit that men deny themselves and bear the cross, if there be no eternal word of truth, which shall support them in their days of darkness and trial?

Mr. Beecher, it is said, attended a banquet with some

noted men in New York. Mr. Ingersoll was among the guests; and some one thought it would give zest to the occasion to have the two famous orators express their views about the Scriptures. Mr. Ingersoll was led to make some ungracious utterance; but Mr. Beecher seemed to take no note. Quietly he began to describe a scene on a crowded street of the lower city. A crippled man, feeble and friendless, leaning heavily on a stout crutch, was trying to thread his way among the reckless teams that pressed along; a burly fellow wantonly knocked the crutch and left the cripple sprawling in filth at the mercy of the wheels and hoofs! As the guests listened with interest and indignation the old preacher glanced at the culprit and sadly remarked: "Mr. Ingersoll is knocking the crutch." The story is impressive, but it is applicable only in part.

Wanton and wicked men, not a few, have assailed the Word; sometimes they have smitten it from the hold of the weak and foolish, who have immediately fallen into the slough; but the truth itself has remained. Voltaire smote it with all the violence of a reprobate life; he sneeringly asserted in a hundred years the book would be forgotten or remembered only as the symbol of an obsolete superstition. Others have assailed the word with every available weapon; they have railed, argued, denounced; they have assumed pedantic airs, and with a conceit that engenders contempt, they have presumed to know more than Jesus or Paul.

Yet the Word abides. As the rain cometh down and the snow from heaven. No form of argument affects the elements. No profanity stops the rain. No blasphemy dissipates the clouds. No criticism, high or low, is heeded by the snow. Floating down upon the still air it drops into its place regardless of what men can do. So shall be the word from the mouth of God. It has come according to the Divine will, and finds expression in all the languages of the earth.

Great societies exist for the whole purpose of multiplying versions and copies; and great scholars spend their best days in rummaging among musty tombs and dusty parchments to discover some new truth concerning that Word. Today it abides in mightier power than ever before; and new copies drop from the press with every tick of the clock.

• *The Word abides because it is true.* Of making many books there is no end, and their perusal is a weariness to the flesh; yet men of real worth drop out of life without so much as an epitaph. They had their victories and defeats; they talked in jest or earnest; but their voices are hushed, and their words have passed away. What words have come to us from beyond the flood? Except a few stray inscriptions repeated at second hand, what have we from the seven ages of Greece? Out of the fullness of their experience they spoke, but their words have passed away.

The cherished theories of science and philosophy have become void with the passing years, because they were founded on error; but the word of God is the truth that sanctifies. It is pure gold unmixed with any baser metal. It is truth in the absolute, a sun without a spot, a glory without shadow.

The Word is abreast of the times; it is abreast of the eternities. Variant interpretations do not affect the truths revealed. Copernicus and his co-laborers utterly destroyed the Ptolemaic system of astronomy and the entire literature of the subject; but they did not touch a single constellation or divert a single orb from its course. Men may change their views of the divine Word, and every erroneous view ought to be changed; but the Word itself is like its Divine Author, it changes not.

• *It abides to meet the necessities of the race.* As the rain and snow from heaven, it watereth the earth. It is seed for the sower, and bread for the eater.

It speaks of God as a Father, who yearns over his erring children, whether among the trees of the garden or by the rivers of Babylon; and to the penitent it offers mercy and pardon.

It gives light to those that sit in darkness and the shadow of death to guide their feet in the ways of peace.

It discovers the balm of Gilead, and the great Physician; and it sings of abounding grace through Him that died and rose again.

It speaks of flocks and herds, of hens and chickens; and it fits into rural life.

It tells of gardens and spices, lillies and palms; and it stirs the interest of those who abide in the tropics.

The cedars of Lebanon fling their shadows athwart its pages, and the splendors of Hermon gleam through its majestic utterances; and it touches the hearts of sturdy mountaineers and the far-off tribes who watch the unsetting sun in the ice-bound realms of the North.

In living imagery it portrays the struggles of fishermen on the Sea of Galilee, or of Paul and his companions on the Adriatic; and it belongs to those who go down into the deep in ships and do business in great waters.

Whether men are prosperous or calamitous, whether they glow with health or waste with disease; whether they hang rejoicing over a cradle or sit weeping by a coffin, they find a message in the Word; and it lives in their hearts.

• *The hopefulness of the Word of God gives it an invincible vitality.* In these days of worldliness and irreverence many are tempted to doubt. Wickedness pervades the earth and infests every rank of society; the scoffer is abroad in the land, breathing out threatening and slaughter against the holiest of things in human experience; and the timid are oppressed. Plain men, who make no claim to learning, and know nothing of manuscripts and versions, they love the Lord; but they hear ominous whispers of treachery and deflection in scholastic circles, and they are afraid. Others seem to despair of the power of the Word in the salvation of the race. But the Word glows with hopefulness. It shall not return void, but it shall accomplish all the divine purpose. It shall prosper in its glorious mission,

> Until the stars are cold,
> And the world is old,
> And the books of the judgment day unfold.

• *I beg you to cherish the word of our God above all other forms of speech.* By taking heed thereto the young man may cleanse his way, and the strong may enhance his strength. Take it to your hearts; it will be a lamp unto your feet, and a light on your paths. Read it in the day of your perplexity, and it will solve your problems. Turn to it in the day of your sorrow, and it will bring you solace. Rest on it in your dying hour, and it will open to you the realms of boundless bliss.

VIII

Father Counsels His Children

IT is the sacred duty of a father to instruct and train his children. The Bible makes this plain by specifically stating that he should "bring them up" (Ephesians 6:4). This parental obligation demands the instilling of the highest and noblest principles in the heart of the child which will build a strong and sturdy character and a useful and wholesome life.

It is the duty of the child to take heed to the father's instructions. The Good Book also points this out: "My son, hear the instruction of thy father, and forsake not the law of thy mother" (Proverbs 1:8).

Now let us hear some of the counsels from a father's heart as he through the years talks to his sons and daughters:

• *Shape your life by a great ideal.* Every person needs something to poetize and idealize his life a little. He needs something he greatly values and which is a symbol of his emancipation from the mere materialism and drudgery of a daily life.

The first step toward realizing a great character is to imagine one. Realization comes after idealization. On an old slate slab in a New England cemetery are these words:

> Think what a good man should be;
> He was that.

It is your fortune to think what good men and women should be, and then be that.

Hawthorne in his story, *The Great Stone Face,* illustrates this principle of how one is transformed into his ideal.

There was on the side of a mountain a clear-cut face. It was said that some day there would come to the village a man resembling the great stone face, and that he would prove to be the people's greatest friend and benefactor.

There was a boy who studied the face of every stranger who came to the valley to see if he might be the one. Time after time he was disappointed. The rich man did not resemble the great stone face. The scholar did not have its features. One followed another as the years passed; but the boy held to the hope that the benefactor resembling the great stone face would come some day to bless them.

As the thought lingered and held sway in the boy's mind he was led to idealize the character of the man who should come. He conceived that he must be lofty in his thoughts, serene in his faith, pure in his character, gentle in his manners and courageous in his convictions. The years went by and his hair whitened and his face took on more and more the internal thought and character of his ideal.

Then the people of the valley came to realize that he was the worthy friend and efficient counsellor of them all, the very image of the stone face.

We become like our ideals.

• *Plan to serve humanity rather than be served.* This is the open road to greatness. The Great Teacher taught that greatness comes through service: "But he that is greatest among you shall be your servant" (Matthew 23:11). He himself "came not to be ministered unto but to minister." Greatness is not found in genealogy, office, wealth or education, but rather in service. The more important aspect of living is not what we get from the world but what we give the world.

Here is a poetic prayer that will help you to cultivate this trait of unselfishness and ministration:

> O Lord, I pray
> That for this day
> I may not swerve
> By foot or hand
> From thy command,
> Not to be served, but to serve.
>
> This too, I pray,
> That for this day
> No love of ease
> Nor pride prevent
> My good intent,
> Not to be pleased but to please.
> —Maltbie D. Babcock

• *Have ambition.* Much mediocrity is not due to a lack of ability, but rather to a lack of ambition. Do not be satisfied to live on the common level just a little higher than a mere existence. Make your plans to achieve. Reach for the higher things. Life is crowded at the lower level, but you will always find plenty of room at the top. Falling short of your ambition is no crime, but low aim is.

> Greatly begin! though thou have time
> But for a line, be that sublime—
> Not failure, but low aim is crime.
> —James Russell Lowell

Little aim and weak endeavor are powerful and severe forces which often shrivel the mind and warp the personality of a person. At first it seems such an innocent view of living; but as fortune passes them by, they often become sour and bitter. Guard against littleness. Keep resentment out of your heart. Remember the shoulders were made to bear burdens, not to carry chips; so never carry a chip on your shoulder. Aiming high plus other requirements can save you from the shriveled soul. Learn to say in the language of the poet:

> Lord, let me not be too content
> With life in trifling service spent —
>   Make me aspire!
> When days with petty cares are filled
> Let me with fleeting thoughts be thrilled
>   Of something higher!
>
> Help me to long for mental grace
> To struggle with the commonplace
>   I daily find.
> May little deeds not bring to fruit
> A crop of little thoughts to suit
>   A shriveled mind.

• *Remember the world has a way of giving back to you what you give it.* There are some exceptions, but generally speaking the principle holds true. You are apt to get as you give.

The Master Teacher expressed this principle of reciprocation in these words: "Give, and it shall be given unto you; good measure, pressed down, and shaken together, and running over, shall men give into your bosom. For with the same measure that ye mete withal it shall be measured to you again" (Luke 6:38).

Love and you will be loved; but hate and you will be

hated. Help others and they will help you. Extend kindness and kindness will come back to you. If you are liberal in dealing with others' imperfections, they will be generous toward your faults; but if you are hypercritical, others will be censorious of you. Be friendly and you will have friends. Solomon said, "A man that hath friends must show himself friendly" (Proverbs 18:24). Smile and the world smiles back at you; frown and the world frowns at you. In other words, life is a mirror.

LIFE'S MIRROR

There are loyal hearts, there are spirits brave,
  There are souls that are pure and true;
Then give to the world the best you have,
  And the best will come back to you.

Give love, and love to your life will flow,
  And strength in your inmost needs;
Have faith, and a score of hearts will show
  Their faith in your work and deeds.

Give truth, and your gifts will be paid in kind,
  And song a song will meet;
And the smile which is sweet will surely find
  A smile that is just as sweet.

For life is the mirror of king and slave,
  'Tis just what we are and do;
Then give to the world the best you have
  And the best will come back to you.
                            —Madeline S. Bridges

• *Be yourself.* You are yourself; therefore you ought to be yourself. This does not exclude self-improvement. Every person should strive to improve, but as himself and not as another. Some have mistakenly thought that in order to place the best foot forward they need to act the role of another. But there is no better way to impress the world than by being genuine, sincere and honest, which are portrayed by being yourself.

> Whatever you are—be that;
> Whatever you say—be true;
>   Straightforwardly act—
>   Be honest—in fact
> Be nobody else but you.

Nothing is gained from imitation. A weaker personality which is yours is much better than a stronger one which is feigned.

> Be no imitator; freshly act thy part;
>   Through this world be thou an independent ranger;
> Better is the faith that springeth from thy heart
>   Than a better faith belonging to a stranger.
> —From the Persian

• *Children, above all be true to self.* Be good to yourself. Like yourself. One reason some people hate others is they actually do not like themselves. They war with others because they have a battle going on within themselves. Anytime you mistreat either acquaintance or stranger, you mistreat yourself. If you should be dishonorable, unfair, crooked, envious, spiteful, unsympathetic or vengeful in your relationship with others, you will hurt yourself most of all. By being true to self, you will not be false to others.

> This above all: to thine own self be true,
> And it must follow, as the night the day,
> Thou canst not then be false to any man.
> —Shakespeare

• *Remember that no one in the long run can really hurt you but yourself.* You can be your best friend or your worst enemy—the choice is yours. If you wage any wars for truth and right, you will have enemies. If you accomplish anything, you will be the object of envy on the part of those whose souls have been shriveled by littleness. Oftentimes the little people who stand about ankle high to tall men will bite at the ankles. It will be annoying and you may be tempted to succumb to despair.

Unscrupulous enemies will start rumors, cast aspersions, spread lies, smear your name, throw obstacles in your pathway, put knives in your back, drive wedges between you and your friends, endeavor to get you dismissed from your employment and interfere with your promotions, all of which is very trying. As the victim of such you are apt to smart and bleed, but you do not have to be defeated by it. At times it will be wise to be silent and passive in the struggle, while at other times it will be smarter to be vocal and active; so your wisdom as well as your courage will be tested. There is no formula for all occasions. When you have to stand up and fight for yourself, you can still do it on the highest plane as a lady or gentleman rather than in the gutter as an unprincipled sniper or a venomous slanderer or an unregenerate calumniator.

> Knowing what all experience serves to show,
> No mud can soil us but the mud we throw.
>
> —James Russell Lowell

A study of both secular and sacred history is encouraging. Even the Bible says, "Woe unto you, when all men shall speak well of you" (Luke 6:26). The pages of history are adorned with the names of many great men and women, but without an exception each had enemies. It seems the greater you become the more enemies you have. But the great arose in spite of their enemies. In many instances the oppositions of the enemies gave them stimuli which enabled them to rise higher, like the contrary winds lift the kite. So a father says, "It is actually up to you." Remember this poem, for it will be a tremendous blessing to you:

> None but one can harm you,
> None but yourself who are your greatest foe,
> He that respects himself is safe from others,
> He wears a coat of mail that none can pierce.
>
> —Henry Wadsworth Longfellow

● *Develop good habits.* Inasmuch as we do many things through force of habit, it behooves us to acquire the best ones. Habit is something that has become so ingrained through practice that it is done regularly and automatically. It is an action so often repeated that it has become a fixed characteristic or tendency.

To illustrate, the chances are you put on first either the left or right shoe without variance every morning. You may go to bed at a certain hour or arise at a certain time because of habit. Habit may enslave you to intoxicants, vile language and many other vices. On the other hand, you may read the Bible, go to church and do many other worthwhile things because of habit.

> All habits gather by unseen degrees;
> As brooks make rivers, rivers run to seas.
>
> —John Dryden

The reason habits are hard to break is that the inclination has been deeply established. So if the habits are helpful, a tenacious and elevating force will be aiding you; but if they are hurtful, a retentive and degrading tendency will lower you.

> Habits are soon assumed, but when we strive
> To strip them off 'tis being flayed alive.

—William Cowper

• *Build your character well.* No matter what your occupation is, you need character to succeed. There can be no success apart from character. The world will test you. You will be subjected to the refiner's fire; and if your character is pure gold, it will shine. On the other hand, if your inner nature is dross, it will be revealed.

Every day you will build a little more on your house of character.

The wise builder builds on a good foundation. No institution, structure or being can be stronger than the foundation. Any house built out of proportion to its foundation will sooner or later fall. The same is true of man. No person can stand out of proportion to his foundation.

A few years ago a business man stated that he needed more room and must get another building. The friend to whom he was talking suggested that he build an additional story on the present structure. The owner explained that years ago when he built his building he had no idea he would ever need more space and thus he did not make the foundation strong enough for an additional floor; and if he should build on it now, the foundation would give way and the building would crumble.

In youth you lay a foundation for life's structure. Years later you may desire to put some heavy, sturdy materials in the structure but the foundation will not support it. This would be tragic. So lay a foundation for life out of such basic elements of character as honesty, integrity, truthfulness, fairness, goodness, sympathy, righteousness and devotion to duty. Then keep building with the best of materials. Build well.

BUILDING

We are building every day
In a good or evil way,
And the structure, as it grows,
Will our inmost self disclose.

Till in every arch and line
All our faults and failings shine;
It may grow a castle grand,
Or a wreck upon the sand.

Do you ask what building this
That can show both pain and bliss,
That can be both dark and fair?
Lo, its name is character!

—I. E. Dickenga

• *Have faith, children.* Faith is a power within that works without. It gives a person the drive to accomplish. Doubts are paralyzing, but faith is stimulating. The more faith we have, the more stimulus we possess. The men and women of faith have accomplished the things doubters have been afraid to undertake.

Our doubts are traitors,
And make us lose the good we oft
might win,
By fearing to attempt.

—Shakespeare

Have faith in God, in man and in yourself. This will keep you from fainting in life's bitter and sweet experiences, and life has both. One of the great men in the Bible said, "I had fainted, unless I had believed to see the goodness of the Lord in the land of the living" (Psalms 27:13). Faith is an antidote to fainting. The determining factor of success in life's sea is neither the tide nor the gale but the faith to see a rainbow in every cloud.

> Who liveth best? Not he whose sail,
> Swept on by favoring tide and gale,
> Swift win the haven fair;
> But he whose spirit strong doth still
> A victory wrest from every ill;
> Whose faith sublime
> On every cloud a rainbow paints—
> 'Tis he redeems the time.

If you would ever find the fortune at the end of the rainbow, have faith; and if you should not find it, that would be fortune enough.

IX

Biblical Rules for Financial Security

ONE of the most strenuous and life-destroying respon-
sibilities of a father is to make a living for his family,
educate his children and leave some sustenance for them
in the event death should cut his life short. There was
a time when this duty was comparatively easy, for a
family would largely live off the land; but today it is different. Today the standards of living are high and the
higher they go, the more demands are made upon father's
energy and managerial qualities. It has never been easy,
but it is a much more laborious task in this age.

In helping man to shoulder this God-given obligation,
we turn to the Bible. The Bible is the greatest book
in the world on economy; because it is a book on living,
and living involves economy. While the Bible teaches
us the principles of living a life, it also teaches us the
principles of making a living. We now point out some
of them:

• *First of all one must have the desire to possess.* "Ye
have not, because ye ask not" (James 4:2). While this
Scripture concerns prayer, it also teaches a lesson on desire. It is obvious that the asking comes from the desire.
The Bible teaches man to both pray and work for his
bread, and in each instance the activity springs from
longing. When the desire for financial security is strong

enough, the necessary conditions will be met to obtain —
with God's help. Personal desire encourages productivity.

• *Reward for labors spurs activity.* "The laborer is
worthy of his hire" (Luke 10:7). Nothing could be fairer
than the principle of more labor, more hire. This is a
strong incentive to work harder. Reward for investments in labor and money will encourage both the
employer and the employee; and business will expand
and everybody will profit.

• *Financial security comes through work.* "In the
sweat of thy face shalt thou eat bread, till thou return
unto the ground" (Genesis 3:19). For us to succeed, there
must be something that puts inspiration into us and takes
perspiration out of us. The Bible is so demanding of
work that it says, "If any would not work neither should
he eat" (II Thessalonians 3:10). It is not often you will
find "pie in the sky"; but if you do, remember somebody
had to bake it. Somebody must work or there will be no
products. The reason some people cannot find opportunity is because it comes disguised as hard work. There
are no elevators in the house of success. You must work
up a step at a time.

Solomon said, "How long wilt thou sleep, O sluggard?
when wilt thou arise out of thy sleep? Yet a little sleep,
a little slumber, a little folding of the hands to sleep:
So shall thy poverty come as one that traveleth, and thy
want as an armed man" (Proverbs 6:9-11).

• *Another requirement for fiscal welfare is self-re-
liance.* You remember the parable of the talents or coins
(Matthew 25:14-20); it shows the necessity of self-con-
fidence. The man with the five coins went forth with

assurance and made five more coins. The man with two coins gained two more. But the one-coin man was afraid and hid his coin. Many people are self-defeated because they do not have faith in themselves. We need to learn that our ship will not come in unless we send it out. Emerson said, "He who thinks success has turned his back on failure."

• *Numbers give strength.*   "Two are better than one; because they have a good reward for their labor" (Ecclesiastes 4:9).   Power can be multiplied through numbers. This principle of strength through numbers accounts for the assembly line and the growth of business in America. We learned that several men working together could produce a finished product in much less time than one working singly. The result has been more products at cheaper prices which led to increased consumption. One has encouraged the other.

• *Vision is a prerequisite to financial success.* "Where there is no vision the people perish" (Proverbs 29:18). It takes vision to see opportunity. It takes vision to see the timely moment.   Opportunity does not bang the door down, walk in and say, "Here I am." If you would appropriate opportunity, you must catch it as it approaches. Oftentimes the very quality that makes the difference between economic success and failure is vision. Some people have it, while others have failed to cultivate it. If you never build a castle in the air, you will never build anything on the ground.

• *Enthusiasm is necessary.*   "Whatsoever thy hand findeth to do, do it with thy might" (Ecclesiastes 9:10). Enthusiasm is another essential in business success. Where there is no real interest, there can be no real success unless it be accidental—which seldom ever happens. Many people have suffered financial ruin because of half-hearted endeavor. In many other cases this was not the contributing factor, but in every instance it was due to the violation of some Biblical principle. A banker friend said, "There is no substitute for brains; but if there could be, it would be enthusiasm."

• *If we would have substance, we must count the cost.* "For which of you, intending to build a tower, sitteth not down first, and counteth the cost, whether he have sufficient to finish it? Lest haply, after he hath laid the foundation, and is not able to finish it, all that behold it begin to mock him, saying, This man began to build, and was not able to finish" (Luke 14:28-30). This is just plain common sense. Because it seems so simple and elementary, many people neglect it—and to their sorrow. Then the refrigerator or automobile is picked up, or the mortgage on the home is foreclosed. It is comparatively easy to start anything, but the strain comes in seeing it through. It is harder to pay a debt than it is to make it. Good business requires sober thinking.

• *The time element is very vital.* "Go to the ant, thou sluggard. Consider her ways, and be wise: which having no guide, overseer, or ruler, provideth her meat in the summer, and gathereth her food in the harvest" (Proverbs 6:6-8). The ant provides its food at the right time. The time element is important to success. There is a time to do things. Solomon said, "To every thing there is a season, and a time to every purpose under the heaven: a time to be born, and a time to die; a time to plant, and a time to pluck up that which is planted" (Ecclesiastes 3:1, 2). A farmer who plants his corn three or four weeks too late is almost sure to see the hot winds scorch it. A merchant who displays his merchandise three or four weeks later than his competitors will lose many sales. It pays to do things that need to be done when they need to be done.

The Bible further states, "Slothfulness casteth into a deep sleep; and an idle soul shall suffer hunger" (Proverbs 19:15).

• *Thrift is another essential requirement.* "Gather up the fragments that remain, that nothing be lost" (John 6:12). Jesus gave this injunction at the time he fed the multitudes. Obediently, they gathered twelve baskets of left-over food. It is a rule of nature that man cannot have by wasting and destroying. He accumulates by producing and saving. Our present civilization is inclined to ridicule this old-fashioned rule of living set forth in the Bible. Whether we appreciate it or not, Christ gave this principle for our good to keep us from destroying ourselves.

Slothfulness and wastefulness are the twin brothers of want. The Bible says, "He also that is slothful in his work is brother to him that is a great waster" (Proverbs 18:9).

• *Wise investments enhance material welfare.* In the parable of talents or coins, we see the value of investments (Matthew 25:14-30). Two investors took savings and invested them judiciously. One gained five talents or coins and another two. We have here a mighty, mighty important lesson for us. Investments have contributed much to our individual and national welfare. When a farmer plants the seed he makes an investment. When a rancher stocks his ranch he makes an investment.

When a man buys a duplex and lives in one part of it and rents the other part, he makes an investment. When several people band together and build a plant and manufacture some product, they make an investment. The good thing about investments is: what you have works for you and does so while you sleep. Investments have contributed much toward making America a great economic giant.

These rules set forth in the Bible will give you financial security. All you have to do is work the rules.

X

Father and Death in the Family

ONE of the bravest and most consoling stories in all the history of man is found in the Bible. The story is one of severe illness and eventual death. It concerns a father and his infant son and the father's helplessness as life slowly ebbed away for his child. All the father could do was fast and pray, and this he did from the depths of his soul with all his might.

That man's name was David. The story is told in Second Samuel, chapter twelve, verses fifteen through twenty-three.

● *Here is the Biblical account:*

> And Nathan departed unto his house. And the Lord struck the child that Uriah's wife bare unto David, and it was very sick. David therefore besought God for the child; and David fasted, and went in and lay all night upon the earth. And the elders of his house arose, and went to him, to raise him up from the earth: but he would not, neither did he eat bread with them. And it came to pass on the seventh day that the child died. And the servants of David feared to tell him that the child was dead: for they said, Behold, while the child was yet alive, we spake unto him, and he would not hearken unto our voice: how will he then vex himself, if we tell him that the child is dead? But when David saw that his servants whispered, David perceived that the child was dead: therefore David said unto his servants, Is the child dead?

And they said, He is dead. Then David arose from the earth, and washed, and anointed himself, and changed his apparel, and came into the house of the Lord, and worshipped: then he came to his own house; and when he required, they set bread before him, and he did eat. Then said his servants unto him, What thing is this that thou hast done? thou didst fast and weep for the child, while it was alive; but when the child was dead thou didst rise and eat bread. And he said, While the child was yet alive, I fasted and wept: for I said, Who can tell whether God will be gracious to me, that the child may live? But now he is dead, wherefore should I fast? can I bring him back again? I shall go to him, but he shall not return to me.

● *Here are some observations from the story:*

The father loved the son with a true unfeigned affection that expressed itself in a profound and unmistakable way.

The father believed in God who was his refuge.

The father understood his own limitations and that he needed help no man could give.

He believed in prayer and was unashamed to pray openly.

He was so overwhelmed with concern for his son that he cared not to eat or sleep.

The father's closest friends misunderstood his strength, serenity and basic view of life and death. The servants feared to tell him that the child was dead, for they feared that he would disquiet himself worse than he had done during the seven days of illness. In this supposition they were wrong.

The father believed in worship; and, when death

came, the first place he went was to the house of the
Lord. His spirit cried out for communion with the Great
Spirit. By recognizing his weakness and the true source
of strength, he became strong.

He knew the possibilities of life.

He knew the finality of death on this earth.

The father had a philosophy of life and death that
could come only to one who had been in touch with
God. He hopefully and resolutely said, "Wherefore
should I fast? Can I bring him back again? I shall go
to him, but he shall not return to me." Never before
had so much been said about two lives and two worlds
in such few words. The statement is one of the gems
of literature. This was the practical view, even though
he surely had to reach down deep into his soul to come
up with such heroism. But he had to be brave — his
position as father would not permit cowardice. The
world loves the brave man.

"I shall go to him, but he shall not return to me"—
these are the words which have been upon the lips of
millions as they turned away from the little mounds in
the silent cities of the dead. They are the tale of man:
his living, his dying, his hope of everlasting life and his
struggles to obtain it. They give purpose to living and
assurance to dying.

• *Rational thinking demands that we believe in the
immortality of man.* Otherwise nothing is permanently
gained. Vegetation springs out of the earth but to die
and to return to the earth again. Animals live, and like
their food, are destined to no higher fate than the enrich-
ment of the earth. Now if this is true of man, if he lives

without a future, then there is no profit in the whole operation of creation. If man lives not beyond the grave, nature labors in vain and toils to no permanent accomplishment. The Creator accomplishes nothing, man lives for no purpose, nature is a stupid and monstrous miscarriage, and the plan of the universe is a stupendous and colossal imperfection. Profound thinking is surely on the side of hope.

• *Our world is a living but dying one.* Everywhere we turn we see life . . . and death. God who does all things well gave us life and then appointed unto the world death.

• *Life in this world without death would be unbearable and impossible.* We cannot have one without the other. Suppose there were no death, no death in the vegetable world, no death in the animal kingdom, no death in the human family — every living thing keeps on living and multiplying. Dense vegetation enmeshes and strangles the whole world. Growing, snapping, biting animals beset us on every side. Human beings are so numerous they have no elbowroom. The old become older; the sick get sicker; the bedridden suffer more; and the broken-hearted are wounded deeper — there is no relief. Think how terrible our world would be. Thank God for death. Thank God that man is not eternal heir to this world. Thank God that man can move into a new world where the wicked cease from troubling and where the weary are at rest.

• *Death was designed to be one of man's most precious blessings.* The Bible says, "Precious in the sight of the Lord is the death of his saints" (Psalms 116:15). And in another place in the Bible we are told, ". . . to die is gain" (Philippians 1:21).

Man's dual nature makes it possible for death to be gain. Man is flesh and spirit, and death is the separation of one from the other. "For as the body without the spirit is dead . . ." (James 2:26). Solomon's oft-repeated statement of comfort further bears out this blessed thought: "Then shall the dust return to the earth as it was: and the spirit shall return unto God who gave it" (Ecclesiastes 12:7).

> I hold that, since by death alone
>   God bids my soul go free,
> In death a richer blessing is
>   Than all the world to me.
>
>   —Scheffler

● *Death is a transitive state.* The Bible says of Rachel, "And it came to pass, as her soul was in departing, for she died . . ." (Genesis 35:18). So death is the means of passing from one world to another one. Death is essential to everlasting life; for "flesh and blood cannot inherit the kingdom of God" (I Corinthians 15:50). These bodies are not suited to an eternal habitation. So it is necessary that we put off the earthly tabernacle that our soul may be clothed with a new body like unto the Lord's own glorious body. Death is merely our transportation.

LAUS MORTIS

> Nay, why should I fear Death
> Who gives us life and in exchange takes breath?
>
> He is like cordial spring,
> That lifts above the soil each buried thing;
>
> Like autumn, kind and brief,
> The frost that chills the branches frees the leaf;

Like winter's stormy hours,
That spread their fleece of snow to save the flowers;

The lordliest of all things!—
Life lends us only feet, Death gives us wings.

—Frederic Lawrence Knowles

● *Responsibility beckons to those who remain in the land of the living.* In a statement upon death and its effects upon those who linger here, coupled with the duties incumbent upon them, Solomon said, "Man goeth to his long home, and the mourners go about the streets" (Ecclesiastes 12:7). This is all they can do — "go about the streets" — and it is natural for those who abide here to mourn, because human ties are strong and sweet. But the world must keep on turning; from the darkness of the night men must look for a new dawn; the broken threads of life must be tied back together with clumsy and shaky hands — in Biblical language, the bereaved must "go about the streets." The hope of immortality dries their tears and heals their hearts. "Concerning them which are asleep," they "sorrow not as others which have no hope" (I Thessalonians 4:13). As sons and daughters of God, they know that if the "earthly house of this tabernacle were dissolved," they "have a building of God, a house not made with hands, eternal in the heavens" (II Corinthians 5:1).

This is our past and present and future all tied up in a nobler plan for man.

Immortality is our hope. It is Biblical. It is rational. It is too necessary not to be true.

● *One of the grandest tributes a father ever paid a deceased son was given by Charles G. Dawes.* The son, Rufus Fearing Dawes, had drowned. The father had been Comptroller of the currency under President Cleveland and had held other high positions. The father's tribute was read by the minister at the young man's funeral, and afterwards was published in booklet form. Among other things, the father said:

"I have taken him with me among the greatest in the nation, and looked in vain for any evidence in him of awe or even curiosity. He has taken me, asking me to help them, among the poor and lowly of earth . . . He did not smoke, nor swear, nor drink. He was absolutely clean. I never saw him angry. In twenty-one years he never gave me just cause for serious reproach. He was absolutely natural in any environment, great or humble. He was extremely ambitious. He was extremely proud. Upon one occasion, years ago, when I mistakenly reproached him, he patiently explained my error, and then peremptorily demanded and received an apology from me . . . My boy lived long enough to 'win out.' Whatever the years would have added would be only material. In a man's character is his real career."

This tribute came from memories. The son was taken, but the father was left a world of precious memories which meant more than the world itself. Our memories are companions and he who has them is not alone. Beautiful memories are helpful friends which inspire man to reach upward to the higher and nobler life.

• *To our dead who have fallen asleep in the Lord, we say:*

Though you have moved on, a lot of you remains here.

To live in the memory of those who love you is not to die.

We shall go to you, but you shall not return to us.

RESIGNATION

There is no flock, however watched and tended,
But one dead lamb is there!
There is no fireside, howsoe'er defended,
But has one vacant chair!

Let us be patient! These severe afflictions,
Not from the ground arise,
But oftentimes celestial benedictions
Assume this dark disguise.

There is no death! What seems so is transition:
This life of mortal breath
Is but a suburb of the life elysian,
Whose portal we call death.

—Henry W. Longfellow